THE Dragon LECTURES

GENE TANNER

The Dragon Lectures
Trilogy Christian Publishers
A Wholly Owned Subsidiary of Trinity Broadcasting Network
2442 Michelle Drive
Tustin, CA 92780
Copyright © 2022 by **Gene Tanner**

Scriptures marked NCV are taken from the NEW CENTURY VERSION: Scripture taken from the NEW CENTURY VERSION®. Copyright© 2005 by Thomas Nelson, Inc. Used by permission. All rights reserved.

For information, address Trilogy Christian Publishing Rights Department, 2442 Michelle Drive, Tustin, CA 92780.
Trilogy Christian Publishing/ TBN and colophon are trademarks of Trinity Broadcasting Network.
For information about special discounts for bulk purchases, please contact Trilogy Christian Publishing.
Manufactured in the United States of America
Trilogy Disclaimer: The views and content expressed in this book are those of the author and may not necessarily reflect the views and doctrine of Trilogy Christian Publishing or the Trinity Broadcasting Network.
10 9 8 7 6 5 4 3 2 1
Library of Congress Cataloging-in-Publication Data is available.
ISBN: 979-8-88738-229-6
ISBN: 979-8-88738-230-2

Chapter One – The Beginning 7

Chapter Two – The Creation Core 17

Chapter Three – The Church. 25

Chapter Four – The Addictions. 37

Chapter Five – The End 43

The Beginning

II Corinthians 11:3, "But I am afraid that your minds will be led away from your true and pure following of Christ just as Eve was tricked by the snake with his evil ways." (NCV)

Revelation 12:9, "The giant dragon was thrown down out of heaven. He was that old snake called the devil or Satan, who tricks the whole world, the dragon with his angels were thrown down to earth." (NCV)

I Peter 5:8, "Control yourselves and be careful. The devil, your enemy, goes around like a roaring lion looking for someone to eat." (NCV)

Scripture is God's inspired word, as it is the main tool He uses to communicating to us today. But the Bible also contains such simple common sense. For instance, what warfare general would go into battle until he knows how many soldiers the other general has?

Luke 14:31, "If a king is going to fight another king, first he will sit down and plan. He will decide if he and his ten thousand soldiers can defeat the other king who has twenty thousand soldiers." (NCV)

Simple, common sense, right?

Is this not also true in sports? No team goes into the game without a game plan based on the other team's weaknesses. Coaches live and die on that scouting report.

This book is designed to be a scouting report. How will our enemy come to us in this day? We all need to be clear on the strengths of our enemy.

We must clearly understand, as we are not engaged in a game, but our warfare is concerning our very soul and eternity. This book aims to lay out the attack of our enemy and conclude, with our defense, leading to complete victory.

THE BEGINNING

This book's goal is not to win nor start a debate, but to get us thinking in ways that may change our outlook, our warfare strategy, and our lives.

Let's begin at common ground. We can all agree that each one of us make thousands of decisions each and every day. Most are decisions we don't even realize we are making. They are a type of muscle memory decisions. Made so fast, without much consequence, that we don't notice them.

Consider, it is getting close to lunch time, I am in my office and the idea comes - should I go to the pizza buffet rather than go home? One decision, right? --no way. Look at what happened in my mind.

1. Should I go for a pizza lunch?
2. I'll go - but should I finish what I am working on and go later?
3. No- I'll go right now.
4. Should I check on what is for dinner to see if I want to pig out?
5. Decide on the time to actually go.
6. There is road work on Main street - should I take a side street instead and go out of my way or take my chances on Main?
7. I'll take main.

8. Should I take the newspaper to read while I eat, or a book?

9. I'll decide on the paper - I can read my books in the office - take a real break.

10. It's hot - should I put air conditioning on or just ride with the window down?

11. Let's go with the air conditioning -but set at what? - let's set at 68.

12. Not many patrol cars around -should I just go five miles over the speed limit, or gun it and take my chances?

13. Should I park in the front by the door or take a parking spot in the back so no one will ding my door?

14. With my newspaper - should I ask for a table by the window for more light to read?

15. At the buffet -- should I begin with a salad and be healthy or go straight to the bread sticks?

16. Bread sticks it is!

17. Order Coke or diet Coke? ---wait, they also have root beer.

18. I've decided to go with root beer.

19. Get the extra parmesan cheese from the waitress or pass on it?

20. Begin with sausage or pepperoni -- or go just cheese?

THE BEGINNING

21. Go ahead and take one of each - the wife is not with me.
22. Should I grab extra napkins or make do with what I have?
23. I'm getting full - should I go up once more and get more pizza?
24. Or should I get a desert pizza slice and call it a day?
25. Was the waitress good?
26. How much of a tip should I give?
27. Were they too busy and the waitress had little time for my table?
28. Should I use the card or just pay cash?
29. Busy road, can I pull out in front of the car coming or should I wait until he passes?
30. Getting low on gas, should I fill up on the way back to the office?

30 DECISIONS OVER A SIMPLE PIZZA BUFFET!

Now I Have A Brand New Set Of Decisions Dealing With The Gas Fill Up!

Okay- little exaggeration but you get the point. Many of these very decisions you will make with a simple trip to a pizza lunch.

If you give me more time, I will come up with a few more decisions you may need to make for this one lunch.

THE POINT --- We make so many decisions each day we may not grasp how many are made -- thousands?

All of our decisions will fall into one of three categories.

1. Holy and in the plan of God for my life,
2. Completely neutral with no bearing on God's plan for my life,
3. A decision that works against God's plan for my life.

Sorry, there is no number 4 - those three encompass every potential decision I will make tomorrow.

The great majority of our daily decisions are neutral. The pizza illustration gives thirty decisions. None of those thirty (although maybe not healthy or best decisions) are neither holy nor sinful.

It is even possible to be wrong - very wrong and have not made a decision that works against God's plan for my life. Driving into Chicago I use the bypass and exit for where I want to go to get into Chicago. Driving around Chicago is so much easier than driving through Chicago.

THE BEGINNING

If I keep missing all the exits and see WELCOME TO WISCONSIN, I have made some really bad decisions. It may be close to impossible to miss all the opportunities to get off the bypass and into the holy land of Wrigley Field. (Be patient, the beloved Cubs will rise again.)

But even so - all those decisions to continue on and ignore all the exits are, of course, neutral.

Wearing socks with sandals - neutral --but that may be evil - gotta check.

With so many decisions being neutral, has our enemy been able to take decisions that are designed to damage our spiritual walk and make them appear neutral? Are there sinful decisions we are making but have been conditioned to believe they are merely neutral? Hence the premise of the book.

Consider, it is the University of Hades (THE FIGHTING DEVILS) the key speaker, the university president himself, is about to speak to the incoming freshman class of demons. The key speaker is none other than that Lucifer, Devil, the Dragon. The class is excited, they will finally see the CEO, the chief, the chairman, the boss, the controller, the head honcho, the kingpin, the commander, the bigwig, the prez, the top dog, the big wheel, Mr. Big himself, the MAN!

THE DRAGON LECTURES

Before The Dragon begins his lecture just a couple of things to notice.

He fears even the name of God, so he will not use

El Elyon

Elohim

Adonai

El Shaddai

Yahweh

Jehovah Shalom

Jehovah Jireh

Jehovah Rophe

Jehovah Mekadesh

Jehovah Tsidkenu

Jehovah Rohi

Jehovah Shammah

He is afraid of even the name. God's name represents all that is holy and worthy of praise, he can't allow himself to honor his enemy with the name of praise. He will refer to the Father as merely, 'The one on that throne.'

THE BEGINNING

He fears the name Jesus, so he will not use

Lord

Jesus

Christ

Son of God

Alpha and Omega

Good Shepherd

Prince of peace

Mighty counselor

I AM

Messiah

Horn of our salvation

Lamb of God

King of Kings

He is afraid of even the name. These names of praise and power will not come from the mouth of Satan. He will refer to Jesus as merely, 'The one on that cross.'

There is an excited hush as they hear his hoofs coming down the hall. The demonic students snap to attention as the dragon enters the room. An evil hush and tension come together as their leader makes his way to the platform. He does not need a microphone; his voice will fill the room with a type of terror.

Seeing the dragon for the first time in person, they are impressed by his size as he takes over the entire lecture hall with his power, but interestingly, they are taken back by his beauty. He certainly can make anything look beautiful. He must surely understand beauty. He must be able to take the most ugly and vile and make it appear to be beautiful.

LISTEN IN -- LET THE LECTURE BEGIN.

The Creation Core

Matthew 7:13-15, "Enter through the narrow gate. The gate is wide, and the road is wide that leads to hell, and many people will enter through that gate. But the gate is small and the road narrow that leads to true life. Only a few people will find that road. Be careful of false prophets, they come to you looking gentle like sheep, but they are really dangerous like wolves." (NCV)

The loud voice streams out and evil words commence.

"Students, you must grasp the creation core. This is the center of our attack. We begin here. Keep in mind the number THREE. It is critical to all creation.

First, it is the basis for 'the one on that throne,' as He is a three in one --Father, Son, and Holy Spirit. His creation is in his image, therefore all human life must also be a three in one --body, soul, and spirit. We will attack all three aspects of the human race.

'The one on that throne' also has a creation narrative and must continue His theme of three, so creation is complete in three parts. These must be understood and destroyed. The creation narrative must be refuted.

The first part of creation is the man/woman event. We attack this by confusing the man /woman distinction. They will become interchangeable. Truth must disappear when humans are able to decide who they are and what they are.

The second part of creation is the marriage event. We must redefine the marriage event. Make marriage a decision of the government and the state and their courts. Simplicity and clarity must disappear. The marriage laws must be defined in any manor the humans desire. The gift of sexuality must be defined as they desire. Fill their passions with the desires we control.

THE CREATION CORE

The third part of creation is the command to propagate and fill the earth event. This must be stopped at the womb level. Turn future life into the lifeless. Turn the most valuable into the most invaluable. Destroy the helpless, but define this as a medical procedure. Do not let humans focus on what is happening within the womb. Control the media and engineer the terms used. Humans gravitate to being in favor of events but reject being against events. Create sentences that use the wording of pro-choice and anti-abortion in the same media sentence. As this is repeated, it will have the subconscious effect we desire.

Should anyone disagree with our narrative concerning these three events, they must be termed as sick with a "phobia." Create a new suffix, "phobic."

Blur the line between acceptance and endorsement within their culture and their churches. Where they believe they are accepting, begin to make them endorse.

Use rage as a tool. Rage can be productive and contagious. Create a selective rage. Have them enraged at what we desire. Is this not clever manipulation.

Bind everything around LOVE. Use love terminology so those who dissent can be seen as unloving. Rhetoric and slogans are important. Create posters wonderfully declaring that LOVE WINS. Who could challenge this?

A young demon stood ---"But sir, we all know that love does not always win. In fact, it tends to lose. Their own holy handbook makes clear that the way to us is wide, but the way to their eternity is narrow. The one with a name we dare not say, let the rich young ruler walk away. He loved him, but on that day, love did not win."

Satan shouted back---"Slogans are important, not facts. We own the world! They will rally around our "truth." We will decide what is correct within the culture; We own the culture. Where there is dissent in the work force, we will send them to enforcement seminars where they will learn our definition of love.

Fear is an important tool to be used. Should they dare counter our narrative, declare it hate speech and therefore must be cancelled or censored. Once a lie is exposed, the only thing left for a power to do is to censor. Use this liberally. Engineer the conversation. Assign virtue to those who agree with our narrative. Used with passion, we will create a cultural intimidation. The culture will fear standing against our narrative.

Redesign reality. Our problem is obvious, knowing, 'the one on that throne' and living in relationship with Him is to truly know reality. This must not be allowed to happen. As we redesign reality, we will demand the world conform to our narrative. No one sins because of self-discipline.

THE CREATION CORE

Our story must be seen as better, our truth must be seen as better, make them believe our lie. We are not the liar, 'the one on that throne' may be the liar. It is vital the culture own our lie, the more a culture moves away from the truth, the more they will hate anyone who dare speak the truth. The truth speaker is now an object of hate. Make them feel good about themselves as they point out anyone who dares speak against our narrative. Declare their words as hate speech. We will now declare what is allowed to be said.

Find damaged people and use them to damage more people. Everything we do is about damage, ruin everything you see and touch. Make those speaking the truth an enemy of the greater culture. This will keep faith issues out of the public square.

Control their focus. Remember, there were thousands upon thousands of trees in the Garden of Eden, but I kept Eve's focus on one single tree. I am the master of focus.

Fill their mind with the focus we desire. Adam and Eve did not want God out of their lives, they just wanted the fruit and God too. Promise them, they can have their own way and God too. This has worked for untold centuries. Teach them, to disobey 'the one on that throne' is without consequences.

Never forget, those easily offended are the easiest to manipulate. Tell them that if they are offended, they must be correct. You cannot be hurt, offended and wrong at the same time. Keep the focus on their own truth. They are comfortable in their own truth. They will be in love with their own truth.

They will be hurt emotionally if their truth is challenged with actual truth. Make them believe that it will only be their own truth that they will be accountable for.

Make emotions more valuable than truth. Their feelings will now be where truth lives. Back to the beginning, wrap their emotions on the three events of their creation, the clarity of man/woman, the clarity of marriage, and the clarity of children."

A young demon stood --- "Master I understand all of our planning and strategy on the creation deconstruction. But they will never buy it. All three are so clear in their holy handbook. On top of that, men were marrying men in Sodom and Lot barely got out alive, they all know this. They won't agree to this again."

Satan roared with a sound that sent all the students trembling back in their chairs. They looked at one another in true fear. "WE OWN THE CULTURE; WE DECIDE WHAT IS REAL AND TRUE! Tell them they can go against God and not be held accountable." The young demon hid his face from their master.

THE CREATION CORE

"Create an US verses THEM mentality, just watch and see who yells the loudest. Use media and politics, both are driven by power and money, two of our most effective tools to corrupt truth. Split their homes and families over issues we want, split their communities, cause riots and chaos over a narrative of our choice. They will battle each other and forget the big picture of 'the one on that cross.'

'The one on that throne' gave humans free will, we will use this to our advantage. Hopefully, they will see only our will and believe it is freedom. Our temporary freedom will damage them eventually. Once the creation event is completely destroyed, all other dominoes will fall quickly and easily.

We do not want them merely telling lies, they need to embrace and live our lies, with all passion.

Reward them when they recite our narrative.

We own the world! I offered all the kingdoms of the world to 'the one on that cross' at His desert temptation, He did not correct me at this point. He couldn't. He knows, that for now, WE OWN THE KINGDOMS AND THE CULTURES OF THE WORLD!

We must press forward in the attack until we lose this power and 'the one on that cross' takes His rightful place. Our time may be short lived, so make the best of it.

NEVER STOP ACCUSING!"

The Church

I John 4:1, "My dear friends, many false prophets have gone out into the world. So do not believe every spirit but test the sprits to see if they are from God." (NCV)

I Timothy 4:1, "The Spirit clearly says that in later times some will fall away from the faith, paying attention to deceitful spirits and the doctrines of demons." (NCV)

"Allow the sleeping giant to sleep.

It is important to make tolerance the key tool here. It is vital to see that love equals tolerance. If I love you, I must tolerate all your behavior and your decisions, therefore, if I can't tolerate your behavior and your decisions, then I don't love you."

At this radical statement a group of daring young demons jumped up, "Sir, tolerance and love are often opposites. Parents love their children but because of their love they don't tolerate all behavior. The one whose name we dare not say - turned over the tables at the temple but loved the merchants. He did not tolerate their behavior and showed His anger at their behavior, yet He still loved them. Tolerance does not equal love and in some instances is the exact opposite."

Satan snarled back, "HOW MANY TIMES MUST I TELL YOU - WE OWN THE CULTURE! THERE IS NO TRUTH IN US! THEY BELIEVE WHAT WE TELL THEM TO BELIEVE!

THE CHURCH

Redesign 'the one on that cross' and have them worship that one. For instance, in our new redesign of 'the one on that cross,' He would have never let the rich young ruler walk away. He would have chased the young ruler and lowered all clear expectations for discipleship. He would ignore the teaching in their holy handbook. He would have chased after the ruler because of our rule of inclusion at all costs. This is the behavior of the tolerant. Inclusion and tolerance are beautiful words, make them beautiful in our image, make those words do what we want.

Perception done well always becomes fact eventually. Propaganda has a singular goal, destroy truth, and create an alternate reality, we must use this effectively.

Continue to blur the line between accept and endorsement. May they begin to endorse behaviors and even celebrate behaviors that we design, but believe they are merely accepting. Consider how culture can now drive the church. Soon the church will desire acceptance and call it evangelism.

Create cowards but call them courageous. If they are merely THINKING of being courageous, are they not cowards? Courage only occurs when they act. Courage is the virtue that unlocks all other virtues. Therefore, courage must be controlled. Keep them asleep, keep them thinking of how to be courageous. As courage disappears, character will follow.

THE DRAGON LECTURES

Someone without character will make no decision for themselves, it will be made for them by the majority. As we control the culture, we will create that majority. When courage and character are gone, not much fight is left in them.

Make them forget the WHY they are following 'the one on that cross.' Turn them into the WHAT. Constantly remind them WHAT they are to do as followers. Get them to merely go to church, finance ministries, volunteer, sing, serve on a board. Doing the WHAT takes their passion away.

The WHAT can turn their journey into chores for 'the one on that cross.' Make discipleship a chore, a list to be completed as an obligation to keep. This is a very different motivation from truly loving 'the one on that cross.' Create believers, not followers. Make them content in their belief.

Keep 'the one on that cross' a respectable distance so that He will have little real influence in their lives. Confine Him to a religion and a religion with chores to be finished in order to be affirmed. Soon, spiritual relationship will be forgotten as affirmation will be the goal.

THE CHURCH

For those not susceptible to our radical suggestions, make them busy. Fill their lives with good things that take time away from 'the one on that cross.' Fight against solitude where 'the one on that cross' may speak into their spirit. Calendar their lives filled with good things. Soon, they may even begin to feel superior to the irreligious.

Brand the follower as zealots and fundamentalists. Once this is agreed to, we can begin to make the claim that they are, in fact, narrow minded, uncaring, and bigots. Branding is important. Never forget, truth is not our core value.

Make them work for their salvation. Now they subconsciously believe 'the one on that cross' owes them something for their hard work. If you earn something, someone certainly owes you something. Let them convert, but only to the religion we design. Soon, they will merely quick read and skim over their holy handbook until they will find verses that validate their feelings. There will be a cynicism to the totality of their holy handbook.

They will invent their own god. They will default to the easy. Create a leadership core in the churches that are not proficient on their holy handbook but somewhat open to suggestion from us. Let our culture begin to design their leadership. Help them modernize to be relevant but lose their core values in the process.

Turn them into victims. Every victim requires a villain. They will always find a villain. Many times, they will make the church their villain. Victimhood will become a currency they will spend liberally. It will make them feel good and find the affirmation they so desire. The more victims we have, the better chance for anger at the churches.

No one can control the past, with its wounds, so use their past, never let them forsake their past hurts. Remind them of every failure, replay it in their soul, embarrass them at the point of their failure, keep guilt at the core of their being. Never let them escape the damage of their past. Do not let them forgive themselves.

They will not see us coming and not recognize our agenda. They will not see that we have been behind their life agenda until it is too late. Never come across as demonic, be cleverer than them.

Help followers to believe that Christian joy exists to solve their problems. Attack at their personal identity -their core - their self interest. This will help reduce prayer to being the problem solver.

Give them what they want, soon they will lose what they need!

THE CHURCH

Soon, when they fall, they will feel that 'the one on that throne' has abandoned them.

They will require meaning and purpose, so, create bondage and call it love and freedom.

Give them permission to achieve their goals in their own way. Create opportunity for their fulfillment to be sought after, in other ways rather than 'the one on that cross.' This will create inner tension.

Hide their inner sadness, dissatisfaction, and frustration under the guise of a false happiness. Help them to find others equally defeated. Help them find each other with social media to validate their dissatisfaction and frustration. Help them cheer each other on in their anger at the church. Victims can always find victims; feed this fire.

Joseph *Goebbels*, our friend and director for propaganda in the NAZI party, told the world, "If you tell a lie big enough and keep repeating it, people will eventually come to believe it." As the lie is heard over and over, it becomes so familiar, it begins to ring true. Repetition will turn a lie into truth. Begin with a simple lie, then build momentum from there.

Let them see me as a myth. Let them see the holy handbook as fables. Santa was a good guy, and I am an interesting and even a potentially scary guy. Make logos of my image with horns and a tail. Make me team mascots. Have me smile. Have me in the crowd making friends. Make me a joke of little influence or threat. I am almost cute and certainly pretty harmless, I cannot be something of terrible power with the ability to ruin lives and families with subtle suggestions. I am not to be one to flee from.

Make the church see that knowledge will set them free, not truth. Let them accumulate knowledge. They will hunger for knowledge, which is not in our plan, but we can still use it. We must control the knowledge they receive and the manor they receive it. Adjust their knowledge to feed into our narrative. Soon knowledge will control them rather than having absolute truth control them.

Urge them to judge everyone by their own strengths and gifts, make this the prism in which they view life. Soon they will seek more gifts rather than the one who gives the gifts. They will unconsciously protect themselves from 'the one on that cross.'

Begin to have them see that 'the one on that throne' is not clear in His holy law. Question His law. Let them believe they can barter with Him.

'Just help my mom get well and I will come to church and quit smoking.'

THE CHURCH

Turn His love, sacrifice and relationship into a negotiation. Turn grace from holy grace graciously given from above to a loved human race, into a blank check.

Strategically, use the most radical 'followers.' These are misguided zealots, so use them effectively. When they hold up signs saying, GOD HATES FAGS at funerals of HIV victims, keep them in the media and social media. Bombard the culture with these images, allow the masses to believe this represents the churches and the work of 'the one on that cross.' Embarrass the movement of 'the one on that cross.'

Humans have a desire for religion, so give it to them. Dominate their world with many different religions for them to invest their passion and faith. Once misdirected, this will direct their spirit away from 'the one on that cross.' Make it clear that in a tolerant society, all religions are equal. Therefore, none have value.

If they put up a sign saying COEXIST, they must be a tolerant and loving person. This person will be honored in the society we create. Pressure them to assimilate into the masses of the religion of tolerance."

A brave demon dared speak up, "But master, their holy handbook makes clear that darkness has nothing to do with light. How can we make them believe that all religions are the same, let alone coexist? If they are to coexist, does this not remove their evangelism? This is becoming so confusing. Why would the followers ignore their own handbook?"

Satan smiled as it was clear this demon has done his homework. "You are correct. We must know the holy handbook; we must know it even better than the humans. When I tempted 'the one on that cross,' I used the holy handbook. So, you use it also, create our interpretations away from the clearest statements.... and yes, we can fulfill their desire for purpose and religion, away from 'the one on that cross.'

Use our *subtlety* to let our culture and narrative creep into their church. Foremost, attack the families. As they are redefined, with our creation narrative, they are now vulnerable. Break down the families. As we, first of all, succeed in the deconstructing of creation, this will be an easy domino to fall.

Their handbook on sexuality is outdated, this does not meet the reality of the world as they now know it. The society has been enlightened. Their holy handbook has requirements that are impossible and even immoral, at the very least, hurtful and dehumanizing. They are no longer relevant to an enlightened society.

THE CHURCH

As the family is outdated, chaos will be another easy goal. Create, encourage this chaos, destroy unity, corrupt everything in your sight. Let their nightly news, each and every night, be about murder, and mayhem until it makes them callous. Make our agenda seem normal until not even the church is appalled."

Help them to be spiritual hypochondriacs, never trusting "the one on that throne" and never resting in Him.

NEVER STOP ACCUSING

The Addictions

II Corinthians 4:4, "The devil who rules this world has blinded the minds of those who do not believe. They cannot see the light of the Good News, the Good News about the glory of Christ, who is exactly like God." (NCV)

Romans 12:1-2, "So brothers and sisters, since God has shown us great mercy, I beg you to offer your lives as a living sacrifice to Him. Your offering must be only for God and pleasing to Him which is the spiritual way for you to worship." (NCV)

Psalm 32:5 "Then I confessed my sins to you and didn't hide my guilt. I said, I will confess my sins to the LORD and you forgave my guilt." (NCV)

George Bernard Shaw "False knowledge is more dangerous than ignorance."

"Always remember, get humans to focus on what we want to them to see. Lot moved near Sodom, but his focus eventually drew him into the city. Focus is always the driving force. Once we have their focus, we give birth to addictions.

Addictions are always based on the NEXT. Therefore, keep that NEXT on the forefront of their minds. Make the NEXT a goal that is achievable and desirable.

The NEXT drink will please and hit that pleasure button I have learned to crave.

The NEXT hand of cards will be a winning hand and give me the thrill I have learned to crave.

The NEXT pornographic video will fit into my fantasy and create the desire I have created in my own mind. Use this to turn women into a commodity rather than the honored place they are to possess.

Keep them focused on the NEXT.

Maintain control of their focus, never let them take their own thoughts captive. Keep their addictions overwhelming them until they give up everything to gain something.

THE ADDICTIONS

Some will be addicted to praise and glory. Press this advantage on leaders, make them accustomed to praise until they expect it.

In addictions, their brain will learn where the comfort and thrill zones are and begin to crave going there. They will be self-taught, and self-wired in their brain. They will have a type of mental muscle memory, racing to where their brain has habitually gone and produced pleasure in the past. This habit will become such an addiction that the brain will fight against changing, as it has always produced a type of pleasure. Even though this is counterfeit, they will still desire this learned feeling.

They will believe this is true happiness. They will eventually give reasons why they deserve this addiction. Humans will believe they control their desires, but now their desires control them. Once mistakenly they believe they are still in control, we have them and now we control their thoughts. They have not taken their thoughts captive, we have.

Continue to engineer the rhetoric, always continue slogans.

Make their problems larger than 'the one on that throne.'

Create heroes for them to emulate, but we control who those heroes will be. Those that follow our narrative more closely, give them all the ammunition necessary to become cultural heroes. Should anyone dare to disagree with our world heroes, make them fundamentally a bad person, not just merely someone with another opinion.

Make them believe that good intentions cover the multitude of sins. Good intentions will always equal being a good person, while there is some truth in this, have them not follow through on their goodness. Let them believe that the good intentions are valuable and enough for 'the one on that cross.' He will certainly honor good intentions. Is there a weaker term than, intent?

Understand and never forget, our enemy is always truth. We must attack this enemy and create an alternate truth. Unfortunately, we must attack a simple fact, TRUTH DOES NOT HAVE FEELINGS! TRUTH IS PURE TRUTH!

So, we must turn this around and create the opposite in their minds.

Convince them that, yes, truth actually does have feelings. Have them start with their feelings and they will build a truth around their own feelings. Therefore, everyone will have a different and personal truth. There will no longer be absolute accountability. This will be my truth and you can have your truth. Their accountability will now be seen around the truth they have created all beginning with their feelings. Have them enjoy their personal truth. Help them to believe they have a moral compass, but it is merely one of their own design. Have humans feel persecuted should anyone challenge their own personal truth.

If you create a trend, you can make it all true for the masses.

We own the world, gain our reward.

Reduce them to living at the mercy of their own misguided ideas, this is the ultimate addiction.

NEVER STOP ACCUSING!

The End

I John 4:7-8, "My dear children, we should love each other, because love comes from God. Everyone who loves has become God's child and knows God. Whoever does not love does not know God, because God is love." (NCV)

I John 8:32, "Then you will know the truth and the truth will make you free." (NCV)

Romans 16:20, "The God who brings peace will soon defeat Satan and give you power over him." (NCV)

"I cannot teach anybody anything, I can only make them think." Socrates

There is a wonderful story concerning a series of events in II Kings.

In short, within the ministry of Elisha, two miracles occur, married to each other. These are particularly germane to this book's topic.

In this period of history, there were the schools of the prophets, a type of seminary of the day.

By the time of Elisha, there were several locations for these schools.

Many are recorded in II Kings, for instance, Bethel in II Kings 2:3, Jericho in II Kings 2:5, and Gilgal in II Kings 4:38.

This miracle story is set in the community of Gilgal.

We must grasp some imagery before getting into the miracles themselves.

Bread often refers to Jesus, as He told us that He was the bread of life.

The broken bread of communion represents the broken body of Jesus on the cross.

II Kings chapter 4 tells us there is a terrible famine in the land.

THE END

No bread was available. It does not require much insight to connect the dots and recognize they also had a spiritual famine. Where there is no bread, it symbolizes there was no Jesus - no God in their land.

There was a spiritual starvation in the entire nation, as well as a food starvation.

They resorted to picking plants to make a stew and mix with some bread grains.

There is a plant that looks like healthy grain but, in fact, was poison. This was not a poison where you get you sick for a couple of days and do not stray from the bathroom, but a deadly plant. Even a small amount could cause your death.

When they picked the plants for the stew, they accidently picked poison and tossed it in the pot with the healthy seeds.

One bite and they knew--- it had a distinctive taste --poison.

They cried to Elisha, the man of God, "Put down your fork and spoon, there is poison in the pot!"

II Kings 4:40 "They poured out the stew for the others to eat. When they began to eat it, they shouted, 'Man of God, there is death in the pot!' And they could not eat it." (NCV)

Elisha's response was to fill it with the grain they had, overwhelm it with grain.

II Kings 4:41, "Elisha told them to bring some flour (grain). He threw it into the pot and said, pour it out for the people to eat. Then there was nothing harmful in the pot." (NVC)

As grain represents Jesus, we are to overwhelm and overflow our poisoned world, for the poison of our world is also deadly, overwhelm our world with the grain of Jesus.

The first miracle, safe to eat the stew, now gives birth to the second miracle.

As there was a famine in the land - and now, there is rumor of a safe stew being served.

Pretty easy to see what happened next.

Surrounding areas of people rushed to lunch.

THE END

Napkins on their collar, fork and spoon in their hands, they came running.

This totaled one hundred men.

It was getting to be a huge picnic for a starving nation.

Our obvious problem, we have a small pot of food designed to feed a few students at the school of prophets.

We can't possibly feed them all with the small amount of stew that we have.

Elisha said to feed them all, there will be more than enough in this small pot.

They kept dishing it out and the pot never ran dry.

On top of this, they had leftovers for the Rubbermaid containers for tomorrow's lunch.

We pick up the story after Elisha tells his servant -- feed them all

II Kings 4:43-44, "Elisha's servant asked, 'how can I feed a hundred people with so little?' 'Give the bread to the people to eat,' Elisha said, 'This is what the LORD says, they will eat and will have food left over.' After he gave it to them, the people ate and had food left over, as the LORD had said." (NCV)

The first miracle, safely feeding the students at the school of prophets despite the poison grains in the pot, because of the bread covering the poison grain.

The second miracle was the feeding of the hundred from such a small pot with even food left over.

It's pretty clear where we are going here. Could our country be in a type of spiritual famine? Are we starving for true bread - starving for Jesus? The real Alpha and Omega, not the counterfeit that Satan has been trying to serve us. Satan's "grain" is a poison that tries to look like true grain, but it is deadly.

Some have taken the false grain and are now frustrated, hurting, and doubting the power of the gospel of Christ.

As so many seek solutions, we live in a world of self-help books. Some may be beneficial for issues such as weight loss. Clearly, a spiritually neutral book and if it helps, good for you. Put down the donut.

But many self-help books begin to try to enlighten with options instead of Christ on spiritual issues. Trying to help the vulnerable find their solution to the spiritual emptiness inside. We desire Christ, anything else leaves us still groping and frustrated spiritually. Some believe, maybe a self-help book will solve my spiritual issues.

THE END

But then again, if I can heal my own self, why do I need Christ?

Why praise God, might as well praise me. I did it!

I may love believing I am completely self sufficient, but it's just not a spiritual truth, but one of Satan's effective lies.

Soon my opinion has eternal value.

Certainly, everyone is entitled to their own opinions.

In fact, I believe all my opinions are true. If I found one that was not true, I would change it. So, as I sit at my desk on this day, I am convinced that all my opinions are true.

But we run into problems when we begin to not merely design our own opinions, but we begin to design our own facts.

We have to be careful not to join the masses. We can't partner in life change if we join the life decisions of the surrounding culture. We are to swim upstream in a culture tending to race downstream.

"When the whole world is running towards a cliff, he who is running in the opposite direction appears to have lost his mind." C.S. Lewis

Never forget, we're the church, never be ashamed of who we are! The gates of hell fear the church. We are on the offensive not on defense running backwards.

Matthew 16:18, "And I say also unto thee, that thou are Peter, and upon this rock I will build my church; and the gates of hell shall not prevail against it." (KJV)

GAME OVER -- THE CHURCH OF JESUS CHRIST WINS!

The issue was ended long ago as Satan was thrown out of God's presence with one third of the angels. The slam dunk occurred on the cross and resurrection on that third day.

God has allowed Satan to rule a rival kingdom, this kingdom of earth. The effects of this are found everywhere, again, just watch your late-night news tonight.

The rival kingdom is dangerous and leads to a disastrous eternity. But this allows us the opportunity of choice. Without a choice, do we really love Jesus? If He is the only option for us, we have no choice, are we not reduced to being robots?

I am thrilled my wife fell in love with me and married me, but if I'm the only man on earth that may not be such a big deal. She chooses to love and marry me. (plus, I am pretty good at begging)

THE END

So here is the meaning of life, choose Christ. Pretty simple!

Everything else is a symptom. How I am as a man, how I am as a husband, father, grandfather, employee - all symptoms? I am on this planet to choose Christ, enjoy Him, serve Him as a follower and have Him receive glory from my life. That is living a kingdom life. No wonder Jesus told us to seek first the kingdom and everything else will be added. (Matthew 6:33) Satan's aim is to rob God of the glory that I was created to give Him. Sin and deception are his weapons, but they are not the end game. They are merely tools, his end game is to rob God of glory, by keeping me from living a kingdom life.

Some may say, I'm not playing. I choose to not be involved. I am not serving Christ, but I am certainly not serving Satan. I make no choices. Sorry, not to choose is to choose. If the glory you were designed to go to Christ is not going to Him, sorry, you have chosen. There are no neutral sites here. This is warfare, with no days off. Satan does not take a vacation nor a day off. There is no neutral Sweden in the spiritual warfare for your soul. At the point of rebellion, Satan is getting glory.

We are told to flee and resist his temptations. The question, as Satan cannot be everywhere, where does he go when we flee? Simple. He goes to anyone not fleeing.

Isaiah 14:13 Satan makes a couple of huge statements. One is that he will go up to heaven. He is not talking about being a tourist. He has been there before, at one point he even had access to God.

Now he is talking - INVASION!

A direct attack on the throne and glory of God. This is personal. He will run things. Every time we act like we are our own creator and run things in our life we are agreeing with Satan. Without realizing it, we are saying, "I will sit on the throne of my life." I will invade my own throne that was designed for God and His glory.

As you read this book you almost feel like there is a war and we are not positive who is going to win? If we all pull on the rope hard enough, who knows, Jesus just might win. That is ridiculous, absurd, asinine, bubble headed, crazy, nutso (have I made my point?).

Satan knows he is out on parole only and has a short time to do as much damage as possible, hence the battle we face today.

Battles yes, undecided war? -NO!

GAME OVER -- THE CHURCH OF JESUS CHRIST WINS!

THE END

So, let's be the church, at all costs.

We live in a world owned by the enemy, and he has filled this pot with poison. Our only alternative is to fill our world with Jesus, overflow the pot with grain.

We must find a way to break down barriers. The church has done well in defining our enemies. We are almost comfortable in calling out our enemies. They are the "others." Some enjoy calling out who our enemy happens to be. In certain arenas some go as far as dehumanizing the "others."

This has been a mistake that we need to fall on our knees before God in forgiveness. This has not advanced the kingdom. But only hurt our cause on a global basis.

Can we begin to reach a world with the clear and graceful love of Jesus.

The world needs to see the selfless love of the church as it is called to be. We are not only to love THE WAY Jesus loves, but also love WHO He loves, this would include those who oppose the work of the kingdom.

The passage at the beginning of this chapter in First John calls us to love. We are to be known by our love. Even more aggressively, if we are not people of love, we are not of God.

Ouch!

Can we love the Muslim and open our arms in Christ style of love?

This is not endorsing - but truly loving.

Can we love the LGBTQ community and open our arms in Christ style of love?

This is not endorsing -but truly loving.

Can we love the powerful people in both media and politics that openly try and oppose the church?

This is not endorsing -but truly loving.

Prove to the world that Jesus is a friend and not an enemy that wants to confine us or damage us. Can we show pure love to those who are hurting or those being fooled by the tactics of Satan?

We are to put on the full armor of God, this is to defeat the enemy of our soul daily. This certainly has a military feel. It makes clear that we are in a war and this war is daily. This is why we must understand the tactics of our enemy.

THE END

Consider the words the Bible uses for Satan

Prince of devils -

Matthew 12:24

Prince of the power of the air - Ephesians 2:2

Ruler of darkness of this world - -Ephesians 6:12

Tempter -Matthew 12:43

Wicked one - Matthew 13:19

Enemy - Matthew 13:39

Accuser- Revelation 12:10

Father of lies - John 8:44

Serpent - Revelation 12:9

Power of darkness - Colossians 1:13

Prince of this world - John 12:31

Liar - John 8:44

Adversary - I Peter 5:8

Angel of bottomless pit - Revelation 9:11

Dragon - Revelation 12:3

Other words describing him are wily, hunting lion, clever, and deceptive.

Did you see the one important word that is missing - STUPID!

Nowhere in scripture is our enemy called STUPID. In fact, it tends to be the opposite. Evil seems to have a type of wisdom.

A perverted wisdom, but a wisdom just the same. He has observed your life, and mine, just to see where our weakness may be. He has observed us from birth. He will use our very strengths against us. He has a clear strategy and play book for me and you. He will use his perverted wisdom to continue to attack at our weakness. No wonder we need to flee and run as close as possible to the presence of the Holy Spirit.

Satan will use his perverted wisdom to attack the church and the Christian culture and influence in the world.

We must understand, respect, and stand clear of our enemy. The great Lord's prayer, "Lead them not unto temptation but deliver them from evil." This was a priority of Jesus as He prayed the great prayer over us.

Ephesians 2:1-2, " In the past you were SPIRITUALLY DEAD because of your sins and the things you did against God. Yes, in the past you lived the way the world lives, following the ruler of the evil powers that are above the earth. That same spirit is now working in those who refuse to obey God." (NCV)

Heavy verse! Gotta chew on this one a bit!

THE END

If you are living outside of God's will you, for your specific life, you are SPIRITUALLY DEAD.

Don't get mad at me, I didn't say it.

If you are not living kingdom, you are spiritually dead. Dead, as in you end up not become unable to respond to Holy Spirit stimuli. Corpses don't function. They don't eat, listen to conversations, interact with others, corpses don't function. - there are plenty of good, moral people who do not function spiritually.

The culture says, "keep your religion to yourselves," but this verse in Ephesians chapter 2 explains why we can't do that. We must awaken ourselves to meet a dead and dying world with life. How can we keep life to ourselves and claim we love those who don't know they are dead?

Satan is temporary. There is no mention of him in the first two chapters of Genesis nor the last two chapters of Revelation. So, we keep our eyes on the prize and the one on the true eternal throne. We strive to see everything through God's eyes. Maybe the great sin is to live our lives as if God does not exist. Does this not lead to all other sins of disobedience?

REMEMBER, SATAN NEVER STOPS ACCUSING

So-o-, finally, the meaning of life is pretty simple, yet so many try to make it complicated. You and I were created so that God would receive glory.

That's it... drop the mic.

Therefore, we are to live each day in such a way that God receives glory in our behavior, thoughts, dreams, and desires. In this way, we defeat the dragon daily. This is seeking first the kingdom.

Now the big question --the hard question - where the Holy Spirit begins to whisper...

ARE THERE DECISIONS THAT YOU BELIEVED WERE NEUTRAL THAT MAY ACTUALLY BE AGAINST THE DESIGN OF GOD AND HIS PLAN FOR YOU TO LIVE A DAILY KINGDOM LIFE?

Long sentence -but it is the reason for the entire book. You may need to read it a couple of times.

Is there even a chance? Has this simple book hit a nerve?

Is there even a chance? Has this simple book made you angry?

THE END

Is there even a chance? Has the Holy Spirit whispered to you over the screams of your enemy?

Messy questions, but necessary.

For your decisions tomorrow, go through the check list.

1. Will this decision give God glory and please Him?
2. Is this decision neutral? (Have I pretended in the past, this was neutral, but I see that it may not be).
3. If the answer to question one and two is NO - back away from the decision.

Make this a habit and your life will change and the trajectory of your entire existence will go up.

Be careful, you are now on the front line of spiritual warfare. Satan does not automatically back up, you must be so close to the Holy Spirit, that he flees. He will back up only if we position ourselves in a manner that makes him back up. Never forget, he fears our Father.

For the record, ... Sorry about the sarcasm that wearing socks with sandals may not be neutral, to keep all truth on the table, it is neutral. But on behalf of the rest of us in all humanity, please cease and desist.

End with GREAT NEWS, God looks with favor on the ones who belong to Him.

> Psalms 34:15, "The Lord sees the good people and listens to their prayers." (NCV)

My prayer is that in exposing the hate and damaging narrative of the evil one that God will receive glory. After all, everything around us is about God receiving glory.

This is our day!

Our world around us is starving for real truth. Let's open our arms in the love of Christ to every hurting person we can come in contact with. Pray daily - God will you put someone in my life for a reason today and give me the opportunity to show them you.

In the beginning of the 34th Psalm, David calls on us to exalt the name of God. This was not just for him; he is urging the reader to join him. He is praising God, but now he invites us to join him. Let us exalt the Father together. He asks us to taste the goodness of God. As we begin to grasp how sweet God is, we will never want to stop singing his praises.

Let us praise and accept the challenges within the word of God for our victory in Jesus's name.

THE END

Ephesians 6:10-12, "Finally be strong in the Lord and in His great power. Put on the full armor of God so that you may fight against the devil's evil tricks. Our fight is not against flesh and blood but against the rulers and authorities and powers of this world's darkness, against the spiritual powers of evil in the heavenly world." (NCV)

Revelation 20:10, "And Satan who tricked them was thrown into the lake of burning sulfur with the beast and the false prophet. There they will be punished day and night forever and ever." (NCV)

Revelation 22:17, "The Spirit and the bride say, Come, Let the one who hears this say, Come! Let whosoever is thirsty come, whoever wished may have the water of life as a free gift." (NCV)

FOR THINE IS THE KINGDOM AND THE GLORY FOR EVER AMEN